Slime

by Jim Eldridge
Illustrated by Rémy Simard

OXFORD
UNIVERSITY PRESS

Chapter 1
The new boy

It was the first day back at the School for Superheroes after the long summer break. In the playground, the children were showing off the new tricks they'd learned. Misha (also known as Mighty Mover) had learned to move huge rocks with the power of his mind.

Lila had learned to make ice waves. "Watch this!" she said.

"Wow!" Misha said, as beautiful waves of ice appeared in front of them.

Hassan (also known as Laser Boy) used his laser eyes to melt the waves.

"Hey!" Lila said.

Lila saw a new boy standing at the edge of the playground, looking lonely. "Hello," she said. "I'm Lila. They call me Freezer Girl. Who are you, and what super skill do you have?"

"My name's Albert," said the boy. "I haven't really got a skill."

"You must have a superpower," said Hassan. "This is a super school!"

"Well, it's not really a superpower," said Albert. "It's more ... I'm just different from other people."

"We're all different," said Misha. "What can you do?"

Albert hesitated. Then he said: "Stuff comes out of my fingers."

"That sounds like me!" said Hassan. "Laser beams come out of my eyes."

"Yes, and I can make ice with my hands!" said Lila. "You're just like us!"

Albert sighed and held out his hands. Slimy, gooey stuff dribbled from the ends of his fingers. It oozed down to the ground and began to spread.

Hassan bent down and poked the goo. "Yuk!" he said. "It's sticky."

Lila scooped up a bit of goo. She dropped it and then smiled as it bounced back up again.

Hassan started to walk away, but he slipped on the goo and fell over. "Stupid goo!" he said, his face red. "I think it's horrible."

"That's just your opinion," said Lila. "I think it's fun."

Lila and Hassan have very different opinions about Albert's goo. Who do you agree with?

"Sorry," Albert said, hurrying over. He tried to help Hassan up, but Hassan didn't want his help.

"Stay away from me, Slime Boy," Hassan snapped, as he got to his feet.

"It was just an accident," Lila said.

Hassan scowled at Albert. "I don't care," he replied.

"He's said sorry, Hassan," Misha said.
Hassan didn't reply. He just stomped off.
Just then, the bell rang for the start of school.

Chapter 2
Asteroid!

Their first lesson was space studies with Professor Powell.

"The professor was the first person to walk on the moon without a space helmet," Lila told Albert. "She can make her own air bubbles."

"Air bubbles are useful," said Albert gloomily. "What good is slime?"

The caretaker made a sudden <u>appearance</u> in the doorway. He looked terrified. "An asteroid is heading for Earth, and it's going to hit here!" he shouted. "It's all over the news!"

Can you pretend to be the caretaker, making a sudden <u>appearance</u> and telling everyone about the asteroid?

"No need to panic!" said Professor Powell. "I'm sure it's just a false alarm." The professor switched on the TV in the corner of the room. The face of a newsreader appeared on screen.

"The asteroid will strike in the next three minutes," said the newsreader. "It will destroy anything it hits! Experts say it will strike right here ..."

A picture of the School for Superheroes appeared on the screen.

"Can we panic now?" asked Hassan.

Everyone got up and ran for the door, screaming and shouting.

Hassan was knocked over in the rush, and Albert ran to help him up.

"Thanks," said Hassan, with a quick smile.

"No problem," Albert replied.

Everyone hurried outside and looked up. They could see the asteroid in the sky. It was just a small dot, but it was getting bigger.

The professor did a quick calculation. She looked over at the playing field. "The asteroid will hit there," she said.

Lila glanced at the playing field, then at Albert. "You can <u>prevent</u> this from happening!" she said.

"How?" asked Albert.

"Make a giant pool of goo on the playing field," said Lila. "When the asteroid hits the goo, it will bounce back into space."

Do you think Lila's plan will <u>prevent</u> the asteroid from destroying the school?

"We've got less than a minute," said Albert. "I'll never be able to run around the field fast enough to create a giant pool of goo."

"You don't have to!" Lila held out her hands. She began to <u>form</u> an icy surfboard. "Jump on!" she said to Albert.

What did Lila <u>form</u> the surfboard from? How do you think they are going to use it?

Chapter 3
The big bounce

Albert hopped on to the surfboard, and they sped off. Lila made icy waves, and they surfed quickly around the playing field. Albert created slimy goo as fast as he could.

Albert looked up and gasped. The asteroid was almost upon them! It was travelling at an incredible speed.

Lila steered the surfboard away as the asteroid shot towards them.

Albert held his breath.

The asteroid hit the giant pool of goo ... and *BOING!* It bounced back into space.

Lila brought the surfboard to a halt. Albert and Lila jumped off and grinned at each other.
"We saved the school!" shouted Lila.
Albert and Lila high-fived one another.

"You did it, Albert!" Misha shouted.

Albert saw the whole school racing towards him. Everyone was laughing and shouting with relief.

"Lila should have a special <u>mention</u>," Albert said. "I couldn't have done it without her."

If you <u>mention</u> something or someone, you talk about them. Why does Albert want to give Lila a *special* <u>mention</u>?

"Well done, Albert," Hassan said. He wanted to make <u>peace</u>. "I'm sorry I called you Slime Boy."

Albert grinned. "It's OK. I sort of like it," he said.

"Hooray for Slime Boy!" shouted Hassan. "Hooray for Freezer Girl!"

To make <u>peace</u> is to end an argument. What else could you say here instead of 'He wanted to make <u>peace</u>'?

Read and discuss

Read and talk about the following questions.

Page 8: Can you think of something that you have a strong <u>opinion</u> about?

Page 12: If someone makes a surprise <u>appearance</u>, does that mean that they are suddenly there, or that they are suddenly not there?

Page 17: Can you think of any other story ideas where Albert and his friends could use their superpowers to <u>prevent</u> a disaster?

Page 18: What happens to water in order for it to <u>form</u> ice?

Page 22: What kinds of things might you give a special <u>mention</u> to after you return from a school holiday?

Page 23: What could you do to make <u>peace</u> with someone you had been arguing with?